Round the Christmas Tree.

A CHRISTMAS TREE

A CHRISTMAS TREE

by CHARLES DICKENS

Pictured in Colour by H·M·BROCK

GUILD PUBLISHING LONDON

This edition published 1969 by
Book Club Associates
by arrangement with Michael O'Mara Books Ltd, London

First impression 1986

ISBN: 0 948397 40 3

Printed and bound by Gráficas Estella, S. A.
Navarra – Spain

A CHRISTMAS TREE

I HAVE been looking on, this evening, at a merry company of children assembled round that pretty German toy, a Christmas Tree. The tree was planted in the middle of a great round table, and towered high above their heads. It was brilliantly lighted by a multitude of little tapers; and everywhere sparkled and glittered with bright objects. There were rosy-cheeked dolls, hiding behind the green leaves; and there were real watches (with moveable

hands, at least, and an endless capacity of
being wound up) dangling from innumer-
able twigs; there were French-polished
tables, chairs, bedsteads, wardrobes, eight-
day clocks, and various other articles of
domestic furniture (wonderfully made, in
tin, at Wolverhampton), perched among the
boughs, as if in preparation for some fairy
housekeeping; there were jolly, broad-faced
little men, much more agreeable in appearance than many real men—and no wonder,
for their heads took off, and showed them
to be full of sugar-plums; there were fiddles
and drums; there were tambourines, books,
work-boxes, paint-boxes, sweetmeat boxes,
peep-show boxes, and all kinds of boxes;
there were trinkets for the elder girls, far
brighter than any grown-up gold and jewels;
there were baskets and pincushions in all
devices; there were guns, swords, and ban-
ners; there were witches standing in enchanted rings of pasteboard, to tell fortunes;
there were teetotums, humming-tops, needle-
cases, pen-wipers, smelling-bottles, conver-
sation-cards, bouquet-holders; real fruit,

made artificially dazzling with gold-leaf; imitation apples, pears, and walnuts, crammed with surprises; in short, as a pretty child, before me, delightedly whispered to another pretty child, her bosom friend, "There was everything, and more." This motley collection of odd objects, clustering on the tree like magic fruit, and flashing back the bright looks directed towards it from every side—some of the diamond-eyes admiring it were hardly on a level with the table, and a few were languishing in timid wonder on the bosoms of pretty mothers, aunts, and nurses—made a lively realisation of the fancies of childhood; and set me thinking how all the trees that grow and all the things that come into existence on the earth, have their wild adornments at that well-remembered time.

Being now at home again, and alone, the only person in the house awake, my thoughts are drawn back, by a fascination which I do not care to resist, to my own childhood. I begin to consider, what do we all remember best upon the branches of

the Christmas Tree of our own young
Christmas days, by which we climbed to
real life.

Straight, in the middle of the room,
cramped in the freedom of its growth by no
encircling walls or soon-reached ceiling, a
shadowy tree arises; and, looking up into
the dreamy brightness of its top—for I observe in this tree the singular property that
it appears to grow downward towards the
earth—I look into my youngest Christmas
recollections!

All toys, at first, I find. Up yonder, among
the green holly and red berries, is the Tumbler with his hands in his pockets, who
wouldn't lie down, but whenever he was
put upon the floor, persisted in rolling his
fat body about, until he rolled himself still,
and brought those lobster eyes of his to
bear upon me—when I affected to laugh
very much, but in my heart of hearts was
extremely doubtful of him. Close beside
him is that infernal snuff-box, out of which
there sprang a demoniacal Counsellor in a
black gown, with an obnoxious head of

hair, and a red cloth mouth, wide open, who was not to be endured on any terms, but could not be put away either; for he used suddenly, in a highly magnified state, to fly out of Mammoth Snuff-boxes in dreams, when least expected. Nor is the frog with cobbler's wax on his tail, far off; for there was no knowing where he wouldn't jump; and when he flew over the candle, and came upon one's hand with that spotted back—red on a green ground—he was horrible. The cardboard lady in a blue-silk skirt, who was stood up against the candlestick to dance, and whom I see on the same branch, was milder, and was beautiful; but I can't say as much for the larger cardboard man, who used to be hung against the wall and pulled by a string; there was a sinister expression in that nose of his; and when he got his legs round his neck (which he very often did), he was ghastly, and not a creature to be alone with.

When did that dreadful Mask first look at me? Who put it on, and why was I so frightened that the sight of it is an era in

my life? It is not a hideous visage in itself; it is even meant to be droll; why then were its stolid features so intolerable? Surely not because it hid the wearer's face. An apron would have done as much; and though I should have preferred even the apron away, it would not have been absolutely insupportable, like the mask. Was it the immovability of the mask? The doll's face was immovable, but I was not afraid of *her*. Perhaps that fixed and set change coming over a real face, infused into my quickened heart some remote suggestion and dread of the universal change that is to come on every face, and make it still? Nothing reconciled me to it. No drummers, from whom proceeded a melancholy chirping on the turning of a handle; no regiment of soldiers, with a mute band, taken out of a box, and fitted, one by one, upon a stiff and lazy little set of lazy-tongs; no old woman, made of wires and a brown-paper composition, cutting up a pie for two small children; could give me a permanent comfort for a long time. Nor was it any satis-

faction to be shown the Mask, and see that it was made of paper, or to have it locked up and be assured that no one wore it. The mere recollection of that fixed face, the mere knowledge of its existence anywhere, was sufficient to awake me in the night all perspiration and horror, with "O I know it's coming! O the Mask!"

I never wondered what the dear old donkey with the panniers—there he is! was made of, then! His hide was real to the touch, I recollect. And the great black horse with the round red spots all over him—the horse that I could even get upon—I never wondered what had brought him to that strange condition, or thought that such a horse was not commonly seen at Newmarket. The four horses of no colour, next to him, that went into the waggon of cheeses, and could be taken out and stabled under the piano, appear to have bits of fur-tippet for their tails, and other bits for their manes, and to stand on pegs instead of legs, but it was not so when they were brought home for a Christmas present. They were all

right, then; neither was their harness unceremoniously nailed into their chests, as appears to be the case now. The tinkling works of the music cart, I *did* find out, to be made of quill toothpicks and wire; and I always thought that little tumbler in his shirt-sleeves, perpetually swarming up one side of a wooden frame, and coming down, head foremost, on the other, rather a weak-minded person—though good-natured; but the Jacob's Ladder, next him, made of little squares of red wood, that went flapping and clattering over one another, each developing a different picture, and the whole enlivened by small bells, was a mighty marvel and a great delight.

Ah! The Doll's house!—of which I was not proprietor, but where I visited. I don't admire the Houses of Parliament half so much as that stone-fronted mansion with real glass windows, and doorsteps, and a real balcony—greener than I ever see now, except at watering places; and even they afford but a poor imitation. And though it *did* open all at once, the entire house-front

Coming home at Christmas time.

(which was a blow, I admit, as cancelling the fiction of a staircase), it was but to shut it up again, and I could believe. Even open, there were three distinct rooms in it: a sitting-room and bed-room, elegantly furnished, and best of all, a kitchen, with uncommonly soft fire-irons, a plentiful assortment of diminutive utensils—oh, the warming-pan!—and a tin man-cook in profile, who was always going to fry two fish. What Barmecide justice have I done to the noble feasts wherein the set of wooden platters figured, each with its own peculiar delicacy, as a ham or turkey, glued tight on to it, and garnished with something green, which I recollect as moss! Could all the Temperance Societies of these later days, united, give me such a tea-drinking as I have had through the means of yonder little set of blue crockery, which really would hold liquid (it ran out of the small wooden cask, I recollect, and tasted of matches), and which made tea, nectar. And if the two legs of the ineffectual little sugar-tongs did tumble over one another, and want purpose,

like Punch's hands, what does it matter?
And if I did once shriek out, as a poisoned
child, and strike the fashionable company
with consternation, by reason of having
drunk a little tea-spoon, inadvertently dis-
solved in too hot tea, I was never the worse
for it, except by a powder!

Upon the next branches of the tree, lower
down, hard by the green roller and minia-
ture gardening-tools, how thick the books
begin to hang. Thin books, in themselves,
at first, but many of them, and with de-
liciously smooth covers of bright red or
green. What fat black letters to begin with!
"A was an archer, and shot at a frog." Of
course he was. He was an apple-pie also,
and there he is! He was a good many things
in his time, was A, and so were most of his
friends, except X, who had so little versa-
tility, that I never knew him to get beyond
Xerxes or Xantippe—like Y, who was always
confined to a Yacht or a Yew Tree; and Z
condemned for ever to be a Zebra or a
Zany. But, now, the very tree itself changes,
and becomes a bean-stalk—the marvellous

bean-stalk up which Jack climbed to the Giant's house! And now, those dreadfully interesting, double-headed giants, with their clubs over their shoulders, begin to stride along the boughs in a perfect throng, dragging knights and ladies home for dinner by the hair of their heads. And Jack—how noble, with his sword of sharpness, and his shoes of swiftness! Again those old meditations come upon me as I gaze up at him; and I debate within myself whether there was more than one Jack (which I am loth to believe possible), or only one genuine original admirable Jack, who achieved all the recorded exploits.

Good for Christmas-time is the ruddy colour of the cloak, in which—the tree making a forest of itself for her to trip through, with her basket—Little Red Riding-Hood comes to me one Christmas Eve to give me information of the cruelty and treachery of that dissembling Wolf who ate her grandmother, without making any impression on his appetite, and then ate her, after making that ferocious joke about his teeth. She was

my first love. I felt that if I could have married Little Red Riding-Hood, I should have known perfect bliss. But, it was not to be; and there was nothing for it but to look out the Wolf in the Noah's Ark there, and put him late in the procession on the table, as a monster who was to be degraded. O the wonderful Noah's Ark! It was not found seaworthy when put in a washing-tub, and the animals were crammed in at the roof, and needed to have their legs well shaken down before they could be got in, even there—and then, ten to one but they began to tumble out at the door, which was but imperfectly fastened with a wire latch—but what was *that* against it! Consider the noble fly, a size or two smaller than the elephant: the lady-bird, the butterfly—all triumphs of art! Consider the goose, whose feet were so small, and whose balance was so indifferent, that he usually tumbled forward, and knocked down all the animal creation. Consider Noah and his family, like idiotic tobacco-stoppers; and how the leopard stuck to warm little fingers; and

how the tails of the larger animals used gradually to resolve themselves into frayed bits of string!

Hush! Again a forest, and somebody up in a tree—not Robin Hood, not Valentine, not the Yellow Dwarf (I have passed him and all Mother Bunch's wonders, without mention), but an Eastern King with a glittering scimitar and turban. By Allah! two Eastern Kings, for I see another, looking over his shoulder! Down upon the grass, at the tree's foot, lies the full-length of a coal-black Giant, stretched asleep, with his head in a lady's lap; and near them is a glass box, fastened with four locks of shining steel, in which he keeps the lady prisoner when he is awake. I see the four keys at his girdle now. The lady makes signs to the two kings in the tree, who softly descend. It is the setting-in of the bright Arabian Nights.

Oh, now all common things become uncommon and enchanted to me. All lamps are wonderful; all rings are talismans. Common flower-pots are full of treasure, with a

little earth scattered on the top; trees are for Ali Baba to hide in; beefsteaks are to throw down into the Valley of Diamonds, that the precious stones may stick to them, and be carried by the eagles to their nests, whence the traders, with loud cries, will scare them. Tarts are made, according to the recipe of the Vizier's son of Bussorah, who turned pastrycook after he was set down in his drawers at the gate of Damascus; cobblers are all Mustaphas, and in the habit of sewing up people cut into four pieces, to whom they are taken blindfold.

Any iron ring let into stone is the entrance to a cave which only waits for the magician, and the little fire, and the necromancy, that will make the earth shake. All the dates imported come from that same tree as that unlucky date, with whose shell the merchant knocked out the eye of the genie's invisible son. All olives are of the stock of that fresh fruit, concerning which the Commander of the Faithful overheard the boy conduct the fictitious trial of the fraudulent olive merchant; all apples are akin to the

apple purchased (with two others) from the Sultan's gardener for three sequins, and which the tall black slave stole from the child. All dogs are associated with the dog, really a transformed man, who jumped upon the baker's counter, and put his paw on the piece of bad money. All rice recalls the rice which the awful lady, who was a ghoule, could only peck by grains, because of her nightly feasts in the burial-place. My very rocking-horse,—there he is, with his nostrils turned completely inside-out, indicative of Blood!—should have a peg in his neck, by virtue thereof to fly away with me, as the wooden horse did with the Prince of Persia, in the sight of all his father's Court.

Yes, on every object that I recognise among those upper branches of my Christmas Tree, I see this fairy light! When I wake in bed, at daybreak, on the cold dark winter mornings, the white snow dimly beheld, outside, through the frost on the window-pane, I hear Dinarzade. "Sister, sister, if you are yet awake, I pray you finish the history of the Young King of the Black

Islands." Scheherazade replies, "If my lord the Sultan will suffer me to live another day, sister, I will not only finish that, but tell you a more wonderful story yet." Then, the gracious Sultan goes out, giving no orders for the execution, and we all three breathe again.

At this height of my tree I begin to see, cowering among the leaves—it may be born of turkey, or of pudding, or mince pie, or of these many fancies, jumbled with Robinson Crusoe on his desert island, Philip Quarll among the monkeys, Sandford and Merton with Mr. Barlow, Mother Bunch, and the Mask—or it may be the result of indigestion, assisted by imagination and over-doctoring—a prodigious nightmare. It is so exceedingly indistinct, that I don't know why it's frightful—but I know it is. I can only make out that it is an immense array of shapeless things, which appear to be planted on a vast exaggeration of the lazy-tongs that used to bear the toy soldiers, and to be slowly coming close to my eyes, and receding to an immeasurable distance.

When it comes closest, it is worse. In connexion with it I descry remembrances of winter nights incredibly long; of being sent early to bed, as a punishment for some small offence, and waking in two hours, with a sensation of having been asleep two nights; of the laden hopelessness of morning ever dawning; and the oppression of a weight of remorse.

And now, I see a wonderful row of little lights rise smoothly out of the ground, before a vast green curtain. Now, a bell rings—a magic bell, which still sounds in my ears unlike all other bells—and music plays, amidst a buzz of voices, and a fragrant smell of orange-peel and oil. Anon, the magic bell commands the music to cease, and the great green curtain rolls itself up majestically, and The Play begins! The devoted dog of Montargis avenges the death of his master, foully murdered in the Forest of Bondy; and a humorous Peasant with a red nose and a very little hat, whom I take from this hour forth to my bosom as a friend (I think he was a Waiter or an Hostler

at a village Inn, but many years have passed since he and I have met), remarks that the sassigassity of that dog is indeed surprising; and evermore this jocular conceit will live in my remembrance fresh and unfading, over-topping all possible jokes, unto the end of time. Or now, I learn with bitter tears how poor Jane Shore, dressed all in white, and with her brown hair hanging down, went starving through the streets; or how George Barnwell killed the worthiest uncle that ever man had, and was afterwards so sorry for it that he ought to have been let off. Comes swift to comfort me, the Pantomime—stupendous Phenomenon!—when clowns are shot from loaded mortars into the great chandelier, bright constellation that it is; when Harlequins, covered all over with scales of pure gold, twist and sparkle, like amazing fish; when Pantaloon (whom I deem it no irreverence to compare in my own mind to my grandfather) puts red-hot pokers in his pocket, and cries "Here's somebody coming!" or taxes the Clown with petty larceny, by saying, "Now, I sawed you

do it!" when Everything is capable, with the greatest ease, of being changed into Anything; and "Nothing is, but thinking makes it so." Now, too, I perceive my first experience of the dreary sensation—often to return in after-life—of being unable, next day, to get back to the dull settled world; of wanting to live for ever in the bright atmosphere I have quitted; of doting on the little Fairy, with the wand like a celestial Barber's Pole, and pining for a Fairy immortality along with her. Ah, she comes back, in many shapes, as my eye wanders down the branches of my Christmas Tree, and goes as often, and has never yet stayed by me!

Out of this delight springs the toy-theatre, there it is, with its familiar proscenium, and ladies in feathers in the boxes!—and all its attendant occupation with paste and glue, and gum, and water colours, in the getting-up of The Miller and His Men, and Elizabeth, or the Exile of Siberia. In spite of a few besetting accidents and failures (particularly an unreasonable disposition in the

respectable Kelmar, and some others, to become faint in the legs, and double up, at exciting points of the drama), a teeming world of fancies so suggestive and all-embracing, that, far below it on my Christmas Tree, I see dark, dirty, real Theatres in the day-time, adorned with these associations as with the freshest garlands of the rarest flowers, and charming me yet.

But hark! The Waits are playing, and they break my childish sleep! What images do I associate with the Christmas music as I see them set forth on the Christmas Tree? Known before all the others, keeping far apart from all the others, they gather round my little bed. An angel, speaking to a group of shepherds in a field; some travellers, with eyes uplifted, following a star; a baby in a manger; a child in a spacious temple, talking with grave men; a solemn figure, with a mild and beautiful face, raising a dead girl by the hand; again, near a city gate, calling back the son of a widow, on his bier, to life; a crowd of people looking through the opened roof of a chamber

Ghost stories round the Christmas fire.

where he sits, and letting down a sick person on a bed, with ropes; the same, in a tempeſt, walking on the water to a ship; again, on a sea-shore, teaching a great multitude; again, with a child upon his knee, and other children round; again, reſtoring sight to the blind, speech to the dumb, hearing to the deaf, health to the sick, ſtrength to the lame, knowledge to the ignorant; again, dying upon a Cross, watched by armed soldiers, a thick darkness coming on, the earth beginning to shake, and only one voice heard, "Forgive them, for they know not what they do."

Still, on the lower and maturer branches of the Tree, Chriſtmas associations cluſter thick. School-books shut up; Ovid and Virgil silenced; the Rule of Three, with its cool impertinent inquiries, long disposed of; Terence and Plautus acted no more, in an arena of huddled desks and forms, all chipped, and notched, and inked; cricket-bats, ſtumps, and balls, left higher up, with the smell of trodden grass and the softened noise of shouts in the evening air; the tree

is still fresh, still gay. If I no more come home at Christmas-time, there will be boys and girls (thank Heaven!) while the World lasts; and they do! Yonder they dance and play upon the branches of my Tree, God bless them, merrily, and my heart dances and plays too!

And I *do* come home at Christmas. We all do, or we all should. We all come home, or ought to come home for a short holiday— the longer the better—from the great boarding-school, where we are for ever working at our arithmetical slates, to take, and give a rest. As to going a visiting, where can we not go, if we will; where have we not been, when we would; starting our fancy from our Christmas Tree!

Away into the winter prospect. There are many such upon the tree! On, by low-lying, misty grounds, through fens and fogs, up long hills, winding dark as caverns between thick plantations, almost shutting out the sparkling stars; so, out on broad heights, until we stop at last, with a sudden silence, at an avenue. The gate-bell has a deep, half-

awful sound on the frosty air; the gate swings open on its hinges; and, as we drive up to a great house, the glancing lights grow larger in the windows, and the opposing rows of trees seem to fall solemnly back on either side, to give us place. At intervals, all day, a frightened hare has shot across the whitened turf; or the distant clatter of a herd of deer trampling the hard frost, has, for the minute, crushed the silence too. Their watchful eyes beneath the fern may be shining now, if we could see them, like the icy dewdrops on the leaves; but they are still, and all is still. And so, the lights growing larger, and the trees falling back before us, and closing up again behind us, as if to forbid retreat, we come to the house.

There is probably a smell of roasted chestnuts and other good comfortable things all the time, for we are telling Winter Stories—Ghost stories, or more shame for us—round the Christmas fire; and we have never stirred, except to draw a little nearer to it. But no matter for that. We came to the house, and it is an old house, full of great

chimneys where wood is burnt on ancient
dogs upon the hearth, and grim portraits
(some of them with grim legends, too) lower
distrustfully from the oaken panels of the
walls. We are a middle-aged nobleman, and
we make a generous supper with our host
and hostess and their guests—it being Christmas-time, and the old house full of company—and then we go to bed. Our room is
a very old room. It is hung with tapestry.
We don't like the portrait of a cavalier in
green, over the fireplace. There are great
black beams in the ceiling, and there is a
great black bedstead, supported at the foot
by two great black figures, who seem to
have come off a couple of tombs in the old
baronial church in the park, for our particular accommodation. But we are not a
superstitious nobleman, and we don't mind.
Well! we dismiss our servant, lock the door,
and sit before the fire in our dressing-gown,
musing about a great many things. At
length we go to bed. Well! we can't sleep.
We toss and tumble, and can't sleep. The
embers on the hearth burn fitfully and make

the room look ghostly. We can't help peeping out over the counterpane, at the two black figures and the cavalier—that wicked-looking cavalier—in green. In the flickering light they seem to advance and retire: which, though we are not by any means a superstitious nobleman, is not agreeable. Well! we get nervous—more and more nervous. We say "This is very foolish, but we can't stand this; we'll pretend to be ill, and knock up somebody." Well! we are just going to do it, when the locked door opens, and there comes in a young woman, deadly pale, and with long fair hair, who glides to the fire, and sits down in the chair we have left there, wringing her hands. Then, we notice that her clothes are wet. Our tongue cleaves to the roof of our mouth, and we can't speak; but, we observe her accurately. Her clothes are wet; her long hair is dabbled with moist mud; she is dressed in the fashion of two hundred years ago; and she has at her girdle a bunch of rusty keys. Well! there she sits, and we can't even faint, we are in such a state about it.

Presently she gets up and tries all the locks
in the room with the rusty keys, which
won't fit one of them; then, she fixes her
eyes on the portrait of the cavalier in green,
and says, in a low, terrible voice, "The stags
know it!" After that, she wrings her hands
again, passes the bedside, and goes out at
the door. We hurry on our dressing-gown,
seize our pistols (we always travel with
pistols), and are following, when we find the
door locked. We turn the key, look out into
the dark gallery; no one there. We wander
away, and try to find our servant. Can't be
done. We pace the gallery till daybreak;
then return to our deserted room, fall asleep,
and are awakened by our servant (nothing
ever haunts *him*) and the shining sun. Well!
we make a wretched breakfast, and all the
company say we look queer. After breakfast, we go over the house with our host,
and then we take him to the portrait of the
cavalier in green, and then it all comes out.
He was false to a young housekeeper once
attached to that family, and famous for her
beauty, who drowned herself in a pond, and

whose body was discovered, after a long time, because the stags refused to drink of the water. Since which, it has been whispered that she traverses the house at midnight (but goes especially to that room where the cavalier in green was wont to sleep), trying the old locks with the rusty keys. Well! we tell our host of what we have seen, and a shade comes over his features, and he begs it may be hushed up; and so it is. But, it's all true; and we said so, before we died (we are dead now) to many responsible people.

There is no end to the old houses, with resounding galleries, and dismal state-bed-chambers, and haunted wings shut up for many years, through which we may ramble, with an agreeable creeping up our back, and encounter any number of ghosts, but (it is worthy of remark perhaps) reducible to a very few general types and classes; for, ghosts have little originality, and "walk" in a beaten track. Thus, it comes to pass, that a certain room in a certain old hall, where a certain bad lord, baronet, knight, or gentle-

man, shot himself, has certain planks in the floor from which the blood *will not* be taken out. You may scrape and scrape, as the present owner has done, or plane and plane, as his father did, or scrub and scrub, as his grandfather did, or burn and burn with strong acids, as his great-grandfather did, but there the blood will still be—no redder and no paler —no more and no less—always just the same. Thus, in such another house there is a haunted door, that never will keep open, or another door that never will keep shut; or a haunted sound of a spinning-wheel, or a hammer, or a footstep, or a cry, or a sigh, or a horse's tramp, or the rattling of a chain. Or else, there is a turret-clock, which at the midnight hour, strikes thirteen when the head of the family is going to die; or a shadowy, immovable black carriage which at such a time is always seen by somebody, waiting near the great gates in the stable-yard. Or thus, it came to pass how Lady Mary went to pay a visit at a large wild house in the Scottish Highlands, and, being fatigued with her long journey, retired to

bed early, and innocently said, next morning, at the breakfast-table, "How odd, to have so late a party last night, in this remote place, and not to tell me of it, before I went to bed!" Then, every one asked Lady Mary what she meant? Then, Lady Mary replied, "Why, all night long, the carriages were driving round and round the terrace, underneath my window!" Then, the owner of the house turned pale, and so did his Lady, and Charles Macdoodle of Macdoodle signed to Lady Mary to say no more, and every one was silent. After breakfast, Charles Macdoodle told Lady Mary that it was a tradition in the family that those rumbling carriages on the terrace betokened death. And so it proved, for, two months afterwards, the Lady of the mansion died. And Lady Mary, who was a Maid of Honour at Court, often told this story to the old Queen Charlotte; by this token that the old King always said, "Eh, eh? What, what? Ghosts, ghosts? No such thing, no such thing!" And never left off saying so, until he went to bed.

A · CHRISTMAS · TREE

Or, a friend of somebody's whom most of us know, when he was a young man at college, had a particular friend, with whom he made the compact that, if it were possible for the spirit to return to this earth after its separation from the body, he of the twain who first died, should reappear to the other. In course of time this compact was .forgotten by our friend; the two young men having progressed in life, and taken diverging paths that were wide asunder. But, one night, many years afterwards, our friend being in the North of England, and staying for the night in an inn, on the Yorkshire Moors, happened to look out of bed; and there, in the moonlight, leaning on a bureau near the window, steadfastly regarding him, saw his old college friend! The appearance being solemnly addressed, replied, in a kind of whisper, but very audibly, "Do not come near me. I am dead. I am here to redeem my promise. I come from another world, but may not disclose its secrets!" Then, the whole form becoming paler, melted, as it were, into the moonlight, and faded away.

A · CHRISTMAS · TREE

Or, there was the daughter of the first occupier of the picturesque Elizabethan house, so famous in our neighbourhood. You have heard about her? No! Why, *She* went out one summer evening at twilight, when she was a beautiful girl, just seventeen years of age, to gather flowers in the garden; and presently came running, terrified, into the hall to her father, saying, "Oh, dear father, I have met myself!" He took her in his arms, and told her it was fancy, but she said, "Oh no! I met myself in the broad walk, and I was pale and gathering withered flowers, and I turned my head, and held them up!" And, that night, she died; and a picture of her story was begun, though never finished, and they say it is somewhere in the house to this day, with its face to the wall.

Or, the uncle of my brother's wife was riding home on horseback, one mellow evening at sunset, when, in a green lane close to his own house, he saw a man standing before him in the very centre of a narrow way. "Why does that man in the

cloak stand there?" he thought. "Does he
want me to ride over him?" But the figure
never moved. He felt a strange sensation
at seeing it so still, but slackened his trot
and rode forward. When he was so close
to it, as almost to touch it with his stirrup,
his horse shied, and the figure glided up the
bank, in a curious, unearthly manner—back-
ward, and without seeming to use its feet—
and was gone. The uncle of my brother's
wife, exclaiming, "Good Heaven! It's my
cousin Harry, from Bombay!" put spurs to
his horse, which was suddenly in a profuse
sweat, and, wondering at such strange be-
haviour, dashed round to the front of his
house. There he saw the same figure, just
passing in at the long French window of the
drawing-room, opening on the ground. He
threw his bridle to a servant, and hastened
in after it. His sister was sitting there,
alone. "Alice, where's my cousin Harry?"
"Your cousin Harry, John?" "Yes. From
Bombay. I met him in the lane just now,
and saw him enter here, this instant."
Not a creature had been seen by any

There comes in a young woman, deadly pale.

one; and in that hour and minute, as it afterwards appeared, this cousin died in India.

Or, it was a certain sensible old maiden lady, who died at ninety-nine, and retained her faculties to the laſt, who really did see the Orphan Boy; a ſtory which has often been incorrectly told, but of which the real truth is this—because it is, in fact, a ſtory belonging to our family—and she was a connexion of our family. When she was about forty years of age, and ſtill an uncommonly fine woman (her lover died young, which was the reason why she never married, though she had many offers), she went to ſtay at a place in Kent, which her brother, an Indian-Merchant, had newly bought. There was a ſtory that this place had once been held in truſt, by the guardian of a young boy; who was himself the next heir, and who killed the young boy by harsh and cruel treatment. She knew nothing of that. It has been said that there was a Cage in her bedroom in which the guardian used to put the boy. There was no such thing.

35

There was only a closet. She went to bed, made no alarm whatever in the night, and in the morning said composedly to her maid when she came in, "Who is the pretty forlorn-looking child who has been peeping out of that closet all night?" The maid replied by giving a loud scream, and instantly decamping. She was surprised; but she was a woman of remarkable strength of mind, and she dressed herself and went downstairs, and closeted herself with her brother. "Now, Walter," she said, "I have been disturbed all night by a pretty, forlorn-looking boy, who has been constantly peeping out of that closet in my room, which I can't open. This is some trick." "I am afraid not, Charlotte," said he, "for it is the legend of the house. It is the Orphan Boy. What did he do?" "He opened the door softly," said she, "and peeped out. Sometimes, he came a step or two into the room. Then, I called to encourage him, and he shrunk, and shuddered, and crept in again, and shut the door." "The closet has no communication, Charlotte," said her brother, "with any other part

of the house, and it's nailed up." This was undeniably true, and it took two carpenters a whole forenoon to get it open, for examination. Then, she was satisfied that she had seen the Orphan Boy. But, the wild and terrible part of the story is, that he was also seen by three of her brother's sons, in succession, who all died young. On the occasion of each child being taken ill, he came home in a heat, twelve hours before, and said, Oh, mama, he had been playing under a particular oak-tree, in a certain meadow, with a strange boy—a pretty forlorn-looking boy, who was very timid, and made signs! From fatal experience, the parents came to know that this was the Orphan Boy, and that the course of that child whom he chose for his little playmate was surely run.

Legion is the name of the German castles, where we sit up alone to wait for the Spectre—where we are shown into a room, made comparatively cheerful for our reception—where we glance round at the shadows, thrown on the blank walls by the crackling fire—where we feel very lonely

when the village inn-keeper and his pretty
daughter have retired, after laying down a
fresh store of wood upon the hearth, and
setting forth on the small table such supper-
cheer as a cold roast capon, bread, grapes,
and a flask of old Rhine wine—where the
reverberating doors close on their retreat,
one after another, like so many peals of
sullen thunder—and where, about the small
hours of the night, we come into the knowledge of divers supernatural mysteries.
Legion is the name of the haunted German
students, in whose society we draw yet
nearer to the fire, while the schoolboy in
the corner opens his eyes wide and round,
and flies off the footstool he has chosen for
his seat, when the door accidentally blows
open. Vast is the crop of such fruit, shining on our Christmas Tree; in blossom,
almost at the very top; ripening all down
the boughs!

Among the later toys and fancies hanging
there—as idle often and less pure—be the
images once associated with the sweet old
Waits, the softened music in the night,

ever unalterable!' Encircled by the social thoughts of Christmas-time, still let the benignant figure of my childhood stand unchanged. In every cheerful image and suggestion that the season brings, may the bright star that rested above the poor roof, be the star of all the Christian world! A moment's pause, O vanishing tree, of which the lower boughs are dark to me as yet, and let me look once more! I know there are blank spaces on thy branches, where eyes that I have loved, have shone and smiled; from which they are departed. But far above I see the raiser of the dead girl, and the Widow's Son; and God is good! If Age be hiding for me in the unseen portion of thy downward growth, O may I, with a grey head, turn a child's heart to that figure yet, and a child's trustfulness and confidence!

Now, the tree is decorated with bright merriment, and song, and dance, and cheerfulness. And they are welcome. Innocent and welcome be they ever held, beneath the branches of the Christmas Tree, which cast no gloomy shadow! But as it sinks into

the ground, I hear a whisper going through the leaves, "This, in commemoration of the law of love and kindness, mercy and compassion. This, in remembrance of Me!"